To Amanda, my shining rock star!
– Mr. Jay

For my loves, Wes, Lana, and Elyse.
– Erin

New Paige Press, LLC
NewPaigePress.com

New Paige Press and the distinctive ladybug icon are registered trademarks of New Paige Press, LLC

ISBN 978-0-578-48389-4

Printed and bound in China

New Paige Press provides special discounts when purchased in larger volumes for premiums and promotional purposes, as well as for fundraising and educational use. Custom editions can also be created for special purposes. In addition, supplemental teaching material can be provided upon request. For more information, please contact sales@newpaigepress.com.

NEW
PAIGE
PRESS

Tess,
the Tin that
wanted to Rock

written by **Mr. Jay**   Illustrated by **Erin Wozniak**

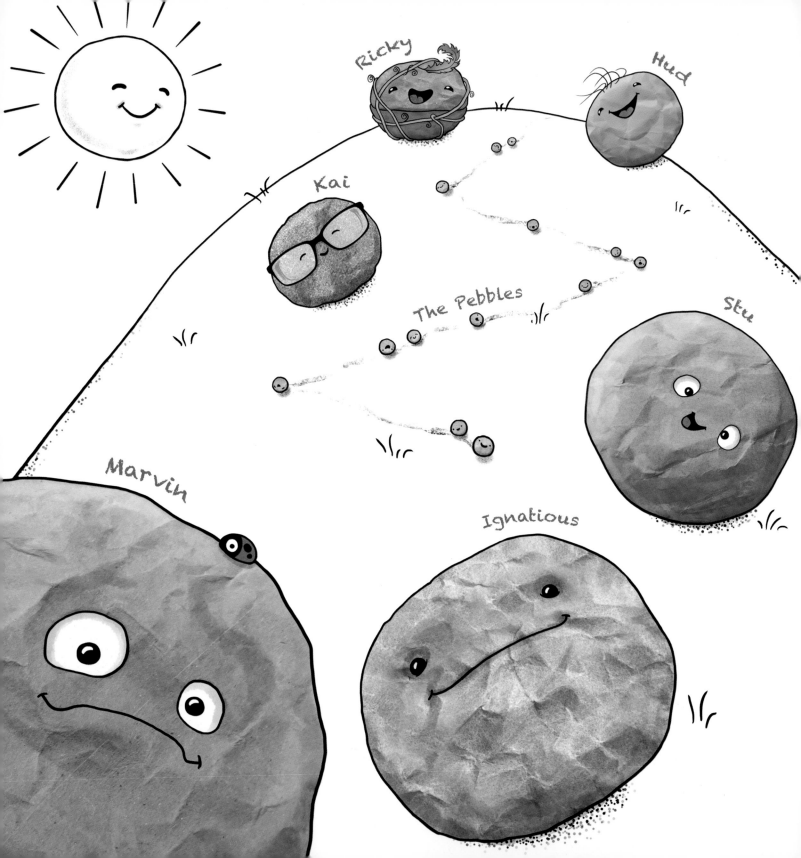

Back at the hill, with the sun high above,
was the group of rock friends that we've all come to love.
Rolling around was the usual crew,
with Ricky and Hud, Kai, Pip and Stu.

Ignatious was playing with Marvin, the Boulder,
as Ebert rolled 'round with a chip on his shoulder.
And Parker and Leesie were chatting away,
while the pebbles zipped 'round in a dizzying fray.

Pip

Ebert

Leesie

Parker

But then, out of nowhere, a new girl appeared,
and the rocks were confused, 'cause she looked kind of weird.
She wasn't that big, not even too tiny...
But they noticed her skin was incredibly shiny.

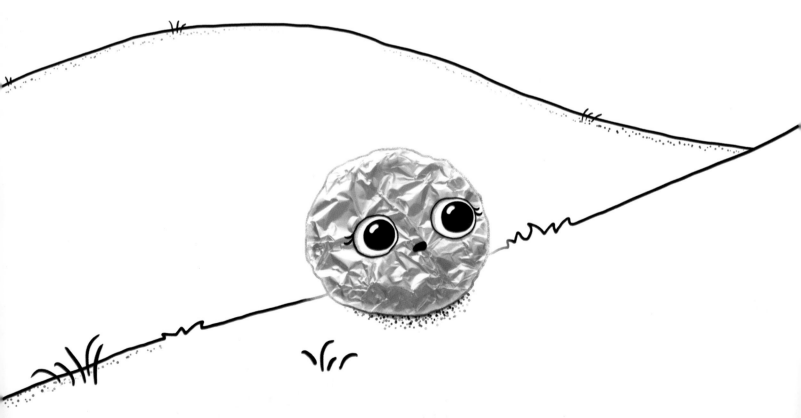

Even so, they were happy to meet someone new,
so the rocks stopped their rolling and said,

"Hi! Who are you?"

The new girl was quiet, and she looked kind of down.
She said, "My name's Tess,
and I'm new here in town.
I've been living inside of a
little boy's pocket,
with a lizard, two coins,
and a broken gold
locket."

"Do you want to play?" asked Parker and Kai.
"No thanks," whispered Tess. "I'm just rolling on by.
I'm sure that you've noticed I don't really fit in.
I'm not even a Rock,
I'm just made of tin.

"I'm not **Smooth** and **Solid**,
and I'm not **Strong** like you...
I'm a **tin foil Ball** –
there's not much I can do."

But just as the rocks had begun their rebuttal,
two pebbles came by in a panicky scuttle.

"Come quick!"

the one yelled,

"It's just as we feared!

Maddy's
out in the forest,
and she's just
disappeared!"

So Marvin, the boulder, then suddenly turned.

"What do you mean?"

he asked, sounding concerned.

"We rolled off the hill
to explore something new -
a beach or a lake
or a tall tree or two.

"Don't fret," Marvin said.
"We'll find her, we will.
But it's not going to happen
                    if we're all standing still!
Come on, let's get rolling, it's what good friends do.
Tess, would you join us?
                    we could use your help, too!"

But Tess just looked sad,

"I don't think I should go.
I'd sure like to help,
    but I roll very slow.
If I go I just know that I'll slow down the pack,
    so I'll stay up on the hill,
        in case she comes back."

Let's look 'round every bend,
and peer down every hole."

And they left, leaving Tess on the hill all alone,
where she teared up and wondered,

"Why can't I be a stone?"

The rocks rolled all day, as the sun left the sky.
Some were tired, some were worried, some just started to cry.
There was no sign of Maddy, they had simply no luck,
when they heard a soft voice up ahead shout,

"I'm stuck!"

It was Maddy! They'd found her – she was trapped in a tree,
in a thick mesh of branches, so they helped her break free.

"Great Job, everyone!"

Marvin said to the pack.

"come on, let's get going,
it's high time we got back."

But which way to go? Which direction was right?
They were lost and confused in the darkness of night.
The rocks didn't know the way that they came,
and out in the distance, all the hills looked the same.

"It's THAT one!"
"No, THAT one!"
"It's the hill on the right!"

"Calm down," Marvin said,
"It won't help if we fight.
Let's head down this way,
along this old trail."

But his voice sounded worried,
and he looked kind of pale.

They asked an old owl, near a bridge that they'd crossed,
who simply confirmed that they were, in fact, lost.
They went down a valley, and around an old cave,
and rolled through a river and over each wave.
They asked a bright flower (who didn't respond),
and got snubbed by a turtle, who dozed by a pond.

More hours passed since they'd started to roam,
out in the wild, and no closer to home.

Then Leesie spoke up:

"Look! A low-hanging star!"

And they all turned to gaze
at the blaze from afar.

On top of one hill something shined very bright -
a shimmering glow in a beam of moonlight.

Marvin smiled.

"That low-hanging star
is our new, good friend Tess.
Her glittering skin
will get us out of this mess.
Come on! Let's head home!
We now know the way.
She didn't think she could help,
but Tess just
saved the day!"

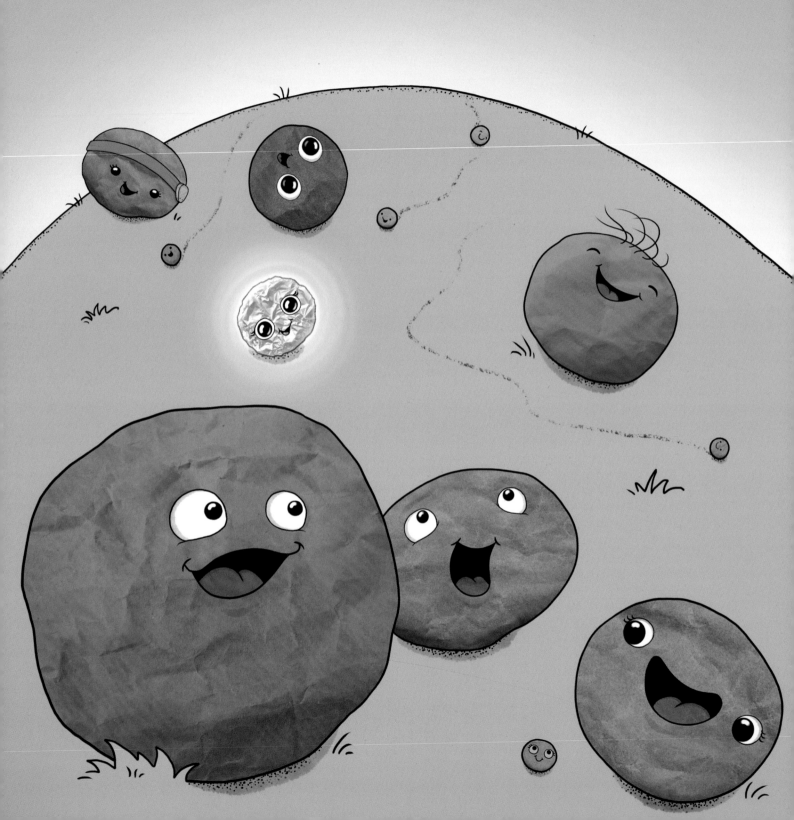

So Bria, the ladybug, who'd been watching with awe,
was bursting with pride at all that she saw,
as the rocks made it back to the hill in the end,
to relay their foray to their tin foil friend:

"You see? You Do matter —
You're important! You are!
You're a tin foil ball,
and our shining
Rock Star!"

About the author
Jay Miletsky

Father, author and business owner, Jay is excited to begin a new career bringing positive, happy and sometimes silly stories to children and their families. He studied economics at Brandeis University, and currently lives in New Jersey, where his daughter Bria Paige is the inspiration for all of his creative writing endeavors.

To book Jay for a speaking engagement and to see his upcoming book titles, please visit jaymiletsky.com or e-mail him at jmiletsky@newpaigepress.com.

About the illustrator
Erin Wozniak

"Erin Wozniak is a creative woman. She teaches kids about art.
She makes paintings, drawing, and stuffed animals, and loves her daughters a lot.
She lives with our dad, who she's married to,
and her two creative and funny daughters (us).
She is having her first time being an illustrator. She is liking it."
-By Lana and Elyse (7 and 5 years old)

To see more of Erin's artwork, visit erinwozniak.com.